Pebble®

Families

Revised and Updated

Brothers

by Lola M. Schaefer

Consulting Editor: Gail Saunders-Smith, PhD

Capstone press®
Mankato, Minnesota

Pebble Books are published by Capstone Press,
151 Good Counsel Drive, P.O. Box 669, Mankato, Minnesota 56002.
www.capstonepress.com

Copyright © 2008 by Capstone Press, a Capstone Publishers company.
All rights reserved. No part of this publication may be reproduced in whole
or in part, or stored in a retrieval system, or transmitted in any form or by any
means, electronic, mechanical, photocopying, recording, or otherwise, without
written permission of the publisher.
For information regarding permission, write to Capstone Press,
151 Good Counsel Drive, P.O. Box 669, Dept. R, Mankato, Minnesota 56002.
Printed in the United States of America

1 2 3 4 5 6 13 12 11 10 09 08

Library of Congress Cataloging-in-Publication Data
Schaefer, Lola M., 1950–
   Brothers/by Lola M. Schaefer. — Rev. and updated ed.
   p. cm. — (Pebble books. Families)
   Summary: "Simple text and photographs present brothers and how they interact
with their families" — Provided by publisher.
   Includes bibliographical references and index.
   ISBN-13: 978-1-4296-1221-0 (hardcover)
   ISBN-10: 1-4296-1221-5 (hardcover)
   ISBN-13: 978-1-4296-1750-5 (softcover)
   ISBN-10: 1-4296-1750-0 (softcover)
   1. Brothers — Juvenile literature. I. Title. II. Series.
HQ759.96.S32 2008
306.875'2 — dc22   2007027026

Note to Parents and Teachers

The Families set supports national social studies standards related
to identifying family members and their roles in the family. This
book describes and illustrates brothers. The images support early
readers in understanding the text. The repetition of words and
phrases helps early readers learn new words. This book also
introduces early readers to subject-specific vocabulary words, which
are defined in the glossary section. Early readers may need some
assistance to read some words and to use the Table of Contents,
Glossary, Read More, Internet Sites, and Index sections of the book.

Table of Contents

4

Brothers

Brothers are boys who have the same parents as other children.

brother

mother

father

sisters

Brothers have brothers.

Brothers have sisters.

Brothers Work

Brothers work together.
Ben and his brother
walk their dog.

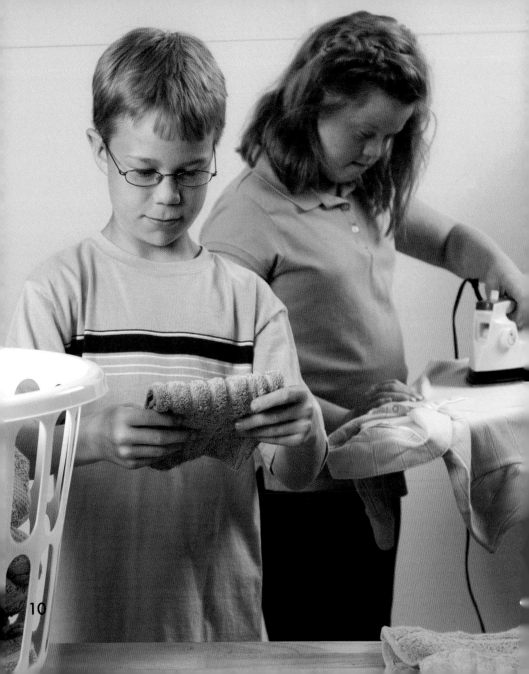

Luke and his sister
help with laundry.

Sam's sister helps him
do homework.

Brothers Play

Brothers play together.
Art and his brother
go fishing.

Chris and his brother
play baseball.

Jim and his sister
blow bubbles.

Orange 'n C

Brothers share.

Glossary

laundry — clothes, towels, sheets and other items that are being washed or that are clean from washing and drying.

parent — a mother or a father of one child or many children; when a parent has more than one child, the children are called siblings.

share — to use something together; siblings often share with each other.

sister — a girl or a woman who has the same parents as another person

Read More

Bercun, Brenda. *I'm Going to Be a Big Brother.* Larkspur, Cal.: Nurturing Your Child Press, 2006.

Dwight, Laura. *Brothers and Sisters.* New York: Star Bright Books, 2005.

Internet Sites

FactHound offers a safe, fun way to find Internet sites related to this book. All of the sites on FactHound have been researched by our staff.

Here's how:

1. Visit *www.facthound.com*
2. Choose your grade level.
3. Type in this book ID **1429612215** for age-appropriate sites. You may also browse subjects by clicking on letters, or by clicking on pictures and words.
4. Click on the **Fetch It** button.

FactHound will fetch the best sites for you!

Index

Word Count: 63
Grade 1
Early-Intervention Level: 10

Editorial Credits
Sarah L. Schuette, revised edition editor; Kim Brown, revised edition designer

Photo Credits
Capstone Press/Karon Dubke, all